DORA the EXPLORER

DORA'S ART ADVENTURE

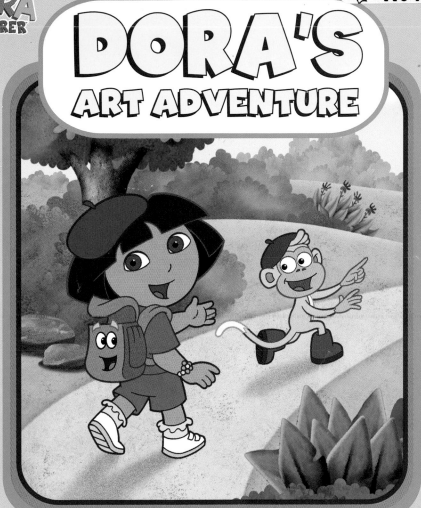

¡Hola! Boots and I are on our way to an Art Fair. Will you help us get there by reading along? Turn the page when you hear this sound.... Are you ready? *¡Vámonos!*

Story Reader

publications international, ltd.

¡Hola! I'm Dora and this is my best friend, Boots.

There's an Art Fair today in *La Plaza*, the Square. Boots and I made some paintings. Now we need to find the way to the Art Fair. Who do we ask for help when we don't know which way to go?

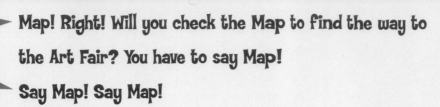

Map! Right! Will you check the Map to find the way to the Art Fair? You have to say Map!

Say Map! Say Map!

I'm the Map! I'm the Map!

Map says we need to go across the Rainbow Valley and through the Colorful Cave. And that's how we'll get to the Art Fair.

Remember: Valley, Cave, Art Fair! Say it with me: Valley, Cave, Art Fair! Let's try to catch stars along the way! Come on! *¡Vámonos!*

First we need to find the Rainbow Valley. *¿Dónde está?*

Where is the Rainbow Valley? Do you see it?

¡Allí está! There it is!

Sí, Azul can help us cross the Rainbow Valley! But wait! Some train tracks are missing! Help us figure out the color pattern so we can put the tracks back together!

¡Roja, amarilla, verde, azul! Red, yellow, green, blue!
We fixed the tracks. Thanks for helping!

Now let's ride across the Rainbow Valley. Chugga chugga choo choo! I hear stars! Do you see stars? Look! ¡Estrellas! There's Artista, the artist star. Artista's painting flowers! I want to catch Artista.

Let's count the stars as we catch them. One, two, three, four! Now let's put them in the Star Pocket. Good star catching!

Yay! We made it across the Rainbow Valley. *Gracias*, Azul.

Now we need to go through the Colorful Cave. Do you see

the Colorful Cave?

There it is! Way up there!

 How will we get up that rocky wall? Maybe there's something in my Backpack that will help us climb. Will you check? You have to say Backpack.

 Say Backpack! Say Backpack!

 Do you see something that will help us climb?

We can use the rope to climb! Good thinking.

Now let's climb up! *¡Arriba!*

Did you hear that? That sounds like Swiper the Fox.

Swiper will try to swipe our rope!

That sneaky fox is always trying to swipe our stuff.

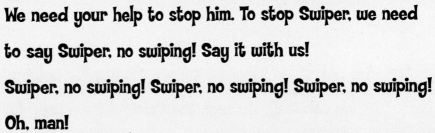

We need your help to stop him. To stop Swiper, we need to say Swiper, no swiping! Say it with us!

Swiper, no swiping! Swiper, no swiping! Swiper, no swiping!

Oh, man!

We did it! We stopped Swiper. Thanks for helping!

We can walk through the Colorful Cave now. Come on!

¡Vámonos!

Look at all the pretty colors in here! We'd better hurry through the Cave. We don't want to be late for the Art Fair.

Yay! We made it through the Colorful Cave. Now we need to get to the Art Fair. But which path should we take? Maybe Artista can help. Let's call Artista out of the star pocket. Artista!

Look! Artista is showing us the path to take! She's painting a rainbow that points the way. *¡Gracias,* Artista! We can follow the rainbow to the Art Fair.

We're at the Art Fair! Hooray! We did it! *¡Lo hicimos!* Now let's go and set up our paintings. Do you see some place we can put them?

Sí, we can put our paintings on the easels.

Look, Boots and I have won blue ribbons for our paintings! Yay!

We had a really exciting trip today.